Time for Little Grover to take a walk!

Pet the puppy.

Baby's First Book™

CTW
SESAME STREET®

Little Grover Takes a Walk

Illustrated by
Tom Brannon

Chase the squirrel.

Swing on the swings.

Feed the birds.

Smell the flower.

Follow the caterpillar.

Time for Little Grover to go home.

6062
ISBN: 0-307-06062-4

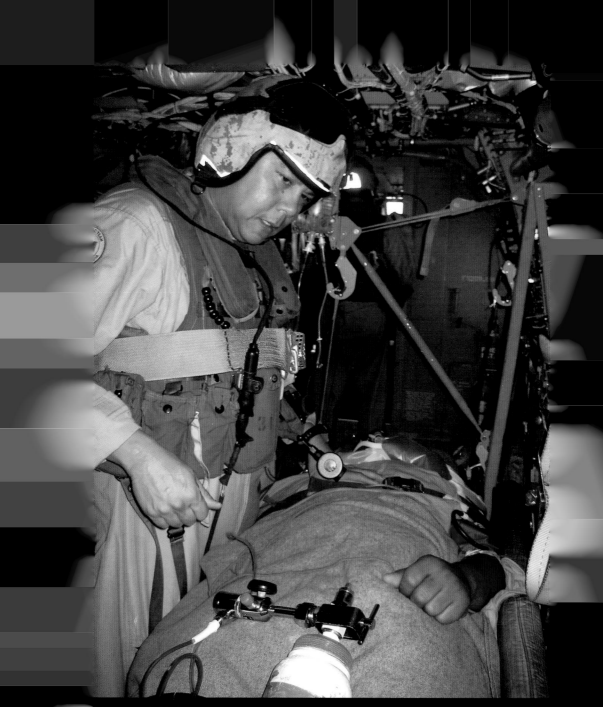

Above: *A U.S. Navy sailor who experienced a medical emergency in 2009 is evacuated by an Osprey.*
Left: *Ospreys are stored aboard the USS* Bataan *amphibious assault ship with their rotors and wings folded to save space.*

V-22 OSPREY FAST FACTS

V-22 Osprey Specifications

Function:	**Transport**
Service Branch:	**United States Marine Corps & United States Air Force**
Manufacturer:	**Bell Helicopter / Boeing**
Crew:	**Three to Four**
Length:	**57 feet, 4 inches (17.5 m)**
Height:	**22 feet, 1 inch (6.7 m)**
Wingspan:	**45 feet, 10 inches (14 m)**
Rotor Diameter:	**38 feet (11.6 m)**
Maximum Vertical Takeoff Weight:	**52,870 pounds (23,981 kg)**
Cruising Speed:	**317 miles per hour (510 kph)**
Ceiling:	**25,000 feet (7,620 m)**
Range:	**879 nautical miles (1,012 miles, or 1,629 km)**

ORIGINS

Tilt-rotor aircraft were very hard to invent. One of the first VTOL aircraft to successfully hover was the Bell XV-3 in 1958. By the early 1980s, the U.S. military chose Boeing and Bell Helicopter to jointly build the V-22 Osprey. Development was long and costly. In 2000, two crashes caused 23 deaths. The program was suspended. Engineers made the aircraft's wiring and electronics safer, and the program continued. By 2007, Ospreys were being used in combat in Iraq.

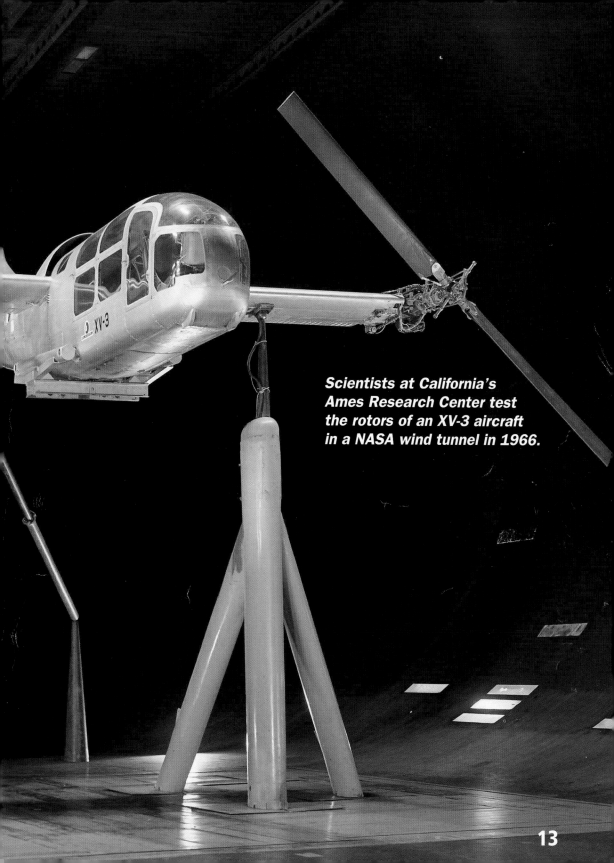

Scientists at California's Ames Research Center test the rotors of an XV-3 aircraft in a NASA wind tunnel in 1966.

VERSIONS

The V-22 Osprey today is used by two military branches. The United States Marine Corps version is called the MV-22. It is gradually replacing the CH-46 Sea Knight helicopter to carry Marines into battle.

Marines and sailors prepare to leave on a training mission on an MV-22 Osprey.

The U.S. Air Force uses the CV-22 version of the Osprey for special operations. It flies long distances into enemy territory. It also resupplies special operations troops, and performs search-and-rescue missions.

NACELLES

Nacelles
(pronounced
"nah-sells")
are the pod-like
structures
on the Osprey's
wingtips. Each
nacelle holds
an engine and
transmission,
and weighs about
7,000 pounds
(3,175 kg).

XTREME FACT

The V-22 pilot controls the nacelles with a small thumbwheel mounted on the aircraft's thrust-control lever.

When the nacelles are up, an Osprey flies like a helicopter.

A hydraulic motor is controlled by the pilot. It turns a giant screw that moves the nacelles up and down. When the nacelles are up, the V-22 flies like a helicopter. When down, the aircraft flies like a plane.

When the nacelles are down, an Osprey flies like a plane.

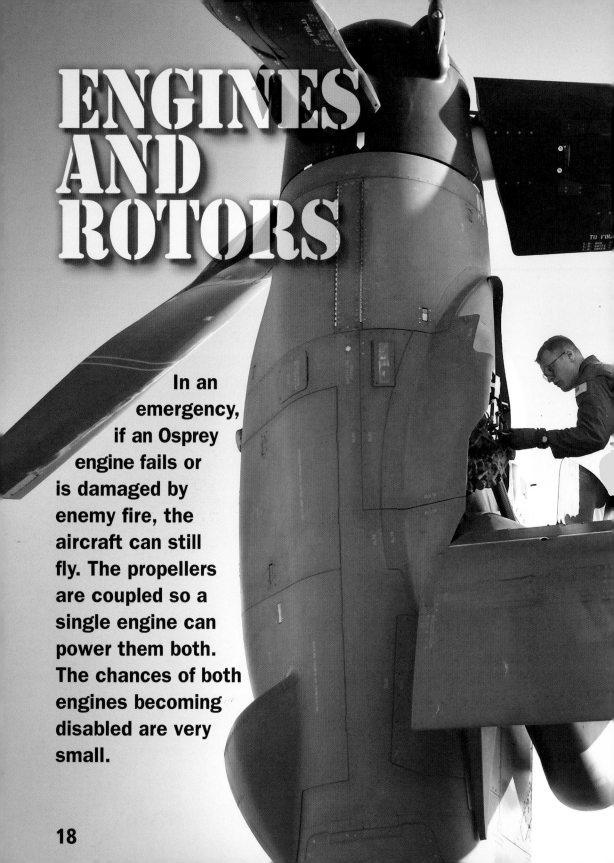

ENGINES AND ROTORS

In an emergency, if an Osprey engine fails or is damaged by enemy fire, the aircraft can still fly. The propellers are coupled so a single engine can power them both. The chances of both engines becoming disabled are very small.

The Osprey uses two sets of three-bladed rotors. They are very large, with a diameter of 38 feet (11.6 m). The propellers rotate in opposite directions for stability.

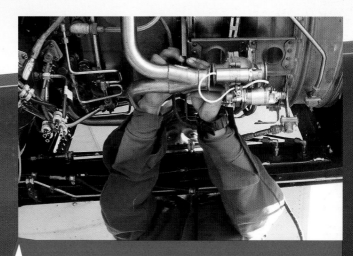

XTREME FACT

Two Rolls-Royce AE1107C engines power the Osprey. They are powerful turboshaft engines, with more than 6,200 horsepower each.

AIRFRAME AND CARGO

The V-22 Osprey is made with layers of carbon fiber. It is a lightweight plastic-like composite material. It is about as strong as steel. It can absorb damage from enemy gunfire or explosives.

At the rear of the Osprey is a loading ramp where troops and equipment enter and exit. The V-22 can carry 24 seated troops with gear, or 20,000 pounds (9,072 kg) of cargo.

XTREME FACT

The Osprey also has a hook-and-winch. It can lift up to 15,000 pounds (6,804 kg) of external cargo, such as artillery or supply crates.

CREW AND COCKPIT

The V-22 Osprey normally flies with a crew of three or four. There is a pilot and copilot, plus one or two crew chiefs or flight engineers. The Osprey has a modern glass cockpit, with LCD displays instead of dials and gauges.

During desert landings, the Osprey's large propellers stir up blinding clouds of dust and sand. Pilots use computers, radar, infrared camera displays, and GPS trackers to help them land safely.

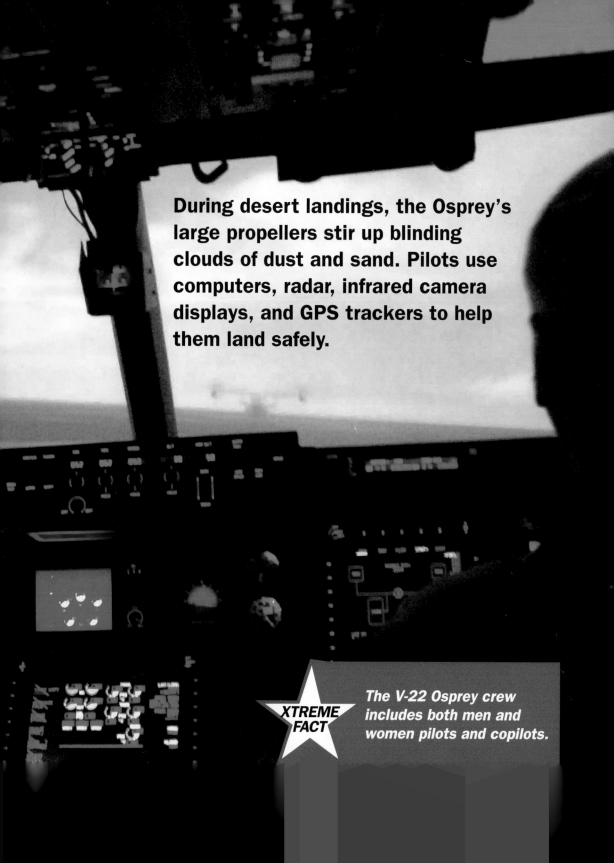

XTREME FACT

The V-22 Osprey crew includes both men and women pilots and copilots.

SELF-DEFENSE

The Osprey is armed
with a single machine
gun. It is mounted on the
rear loading ramp. The weapon
can be either a 7.62 mm M240 or
.50 caliber M2 Browning machine gun.
There are plans to add a second gun that
can fire forward in all directions.
Some Ospreys already are armed
with a GAU-17 Gatling-style gun.
This retractable weapon is
mounted under the aircraft's
belly. It is fired remotely
by the copilot.

A Marine operates a V-22 Osprey's M240 machine gun in the skies over Afghanistan.

XTREME FACT

Computers monitoring the belly-mounted GAU-17 prevent it from accidentally shooting the Osprey's landing gear or rotors.

Slow-moving helicopters are vulnerable to attack from firearms and rocket propelled grenades. The V-22 Osprey can fly faster and higher than any helicopter, which helps protect it from harm. The Osprey also has defense against heat-seeking missiles. Its engine exhaust is cooled. This reduces the aircraft's heat signature. The V-22 can also fire defensive flares to fool enemy heat-seeking missiles.

A V-22 Osprey fires flares in a training mission over California.

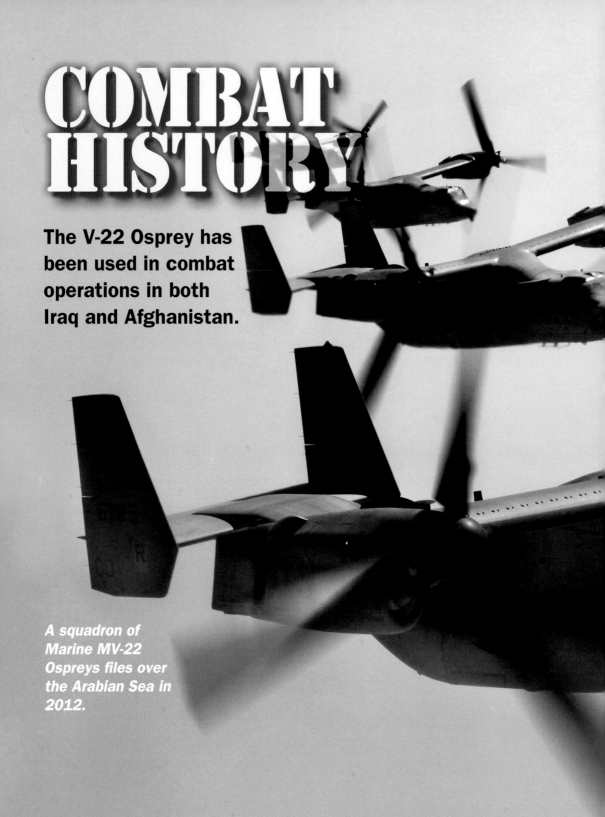

COMBAT HISTORY

The V-22 Osprey has been used in combat operations in both Iraq and Afghanistan.

A squadron of Marine MV-22 Ospreys files over the Arabian Sea in 2012.

After hundreds
of missions,
the Osprey has
proven a reliable
workhorse. Its speed
and range allow
troops and cargo to
be transported much
more effectively than by
helicopter.

XTREME FACT

The first combat squadron of V-22 Ospreys was deployed to Iraq in September 2007. The squadron's nickname is "The Thunder Chickens."

GLOSSARY

AIRFRAME

The body of an aircraft, minus its engine.

COMPOSITE

A strong, lightweight material that blends two or more elements, such as plastic and ceramic resins. Fiberglass and Kevlar are two kinds of composite materials.

FLARE

A device used by aircraft to fool heat-seeking missiles. Flares are "countermeasures." When a surface-to-air or air-to-air heat-seeking missile is fired, it most commonly detects hot exhaust gasses from an aircraft's engines. If the aircraft detects the heat-seeking missile in time, it releases one or more flares into the air. Flares are made of hot-burning metals, like magnesium. When ignited, they burn at a temperature equal to the aircraft's engines, sometimes even hotter. Heat-seeking missiles often detect the flare and then veer away from the aircraft, giving the aircraft time to fly safely away.

GPS (GLOBAL POSITIONING SYSTEM)

A system of orbiting satellites that transmits information to GPS receivers on Earth. Using information from the satellites, receivers can calculate location, speed, and direction with great accuracy.

NAUTICAL MILE

A standard way to measure distance, especially when traveling in an aircraft or ship. It is based on the circumference of the Earth, the distance around

the equator. This large circle is divided into 360 degrees. Each degree is further divided into 60 units called "minutes." A single minute of arc around the Earth is one nautical mile.

Radar

A way to detect objects, such as aircraft or ships, using electromagnetic (radio) waves. Radar waves are sent out by large dishes, or antennas, and then strike an object. The radar dish then detects the reflected wave, which can tell operators how big an object is, how fast it is moving, its altitude, and its direction.

Special Forces

Very highly trained soldiers who perform unusual or risky missions. They are usually organized in small groups and use stealth, speed, and surprise to achieve their objectives. Special operations soldiers are very self reliant while performing their missions.

VTOL (Vertical Take-Off and Landing)

A unique aircraft, usually other than a helicopter, that can takeoff and land vertically. A V-22 Osprey is a VTOL aircraft.

INDEX